I Dream of A'maresh

(A Post-Nuclear Tragedy)

Written and Illustrated

By

Allen F. McNair

--A Reality Check Production--

I Dream of A'maresh™

Book II

(A Post-Nuclear Tragedy)

Written and Illustrated

By

Allen F. McNair

Reality Check Publications
2303 N. Clybourn Avenue
Apt. No. 2A
Chicago, Illinois 60614

I Dream of A'maresh

I DREAM OF A'MARESH:

BOOK I

TABLE OF CONTENTS

TABLE OF CONTENTS

TABLE OF CONTENTS

I Dream of A'maresh

I Dream of A'maresh

Prologue: An Author's Dream of A'maresh

In 1967, I dream of A'maresh, a lovely and noble lady
From farthest shore, over a celestial sea, a large romance.
I dream of a huge holocaust, of nuclear proportions,
Devastating and ravishing huge metropolises forever.

In my dream a more peaceful, pastoral world emerges.
A brave hero discovers a tender maiden in forest glen.
Love blossoms and soon, a family gets created from it.
A lovely and buxom daughter is born to the two lovers.

But tragedy all too soon strikes the three innocents.
An illness peculiar to only A'maresh strikes her.
This entire momentous occurrence happens in my dream.
The grief of husband and daughter strikes my heart.

Upon awaking from the dream, I want to tell the story.
But years pass before maturity of my experience allows me
The muse and creative platform to tell the rich tale fully.
In 1991, the format of poetry and illustrative art permit me.

A great burst of generous energy compels me to write,
A tremendous need for expression leads me to draw.
Details for the tale, before unavailable to me, rush to me.
Characters, previously unrevealed to me, come to mind.

In eleven days, I print out a full story, with art included the
Next year. Sixteen poems of epic proportions emerge readily.
Flushed with relief, I thought the story was complete.
Twenty-five years seemed to be a long, loving birthing process.

I revealed my story to a select few, who wondered at it.
The concept to them seemed hard to grasp or appreciate.
The magical tale seemed to hold magic only for me.
I put the whole project on a shelf marked "Oblivion."

I Dream of A'maresh

Fourteen years later, I met with some encouragement.
A remarkable woman carefully read this epic adventure.
Her questions and insights renewed my energy and motivation.
I was recharged to examine the giant work and write anew.

Five new chapters became seven to expand and revitalize this epic.
Revisions came to clarify certain points of the story's plot.
Verses written anew helped to bring sharper focus to new story.
Added text clarified obscure passages to improve overall design.

It is my wish to entertain and enlighten my readers' imagination.
This beautiful story in its present form is my greatest delight.
I hope it will reflect increased maturity in its new telling.
I also hope the readers will enjoy it as much as I love relating it.

4/03/05
Revised 07/27/12

An Author's Dream

Shadows, Now Impacted

<u>Of Wrath More Powerful</u>

Sirens scream two minute
Warning as end rushes in.
People falling down black
Stairwells, trampling others.

Animal faces of human masks,
Hands clawing on last worldly
Goods, their own and not theirs,
They run, blindly, to nowhere.

Inhuman acts more horrible
Than impending doom of death
In civilization's tall monuments.
Smoky mushroom's first landfall

Tells of wrath more powerful than
God's own thunder-stroke. Death,
Destruction instant beneath cloud
And swift, hot fireball unchecked.

Broken wall, blackened by shadows,
Impacted by children who once
Played ball, hopscotch, and jumped
Rope to lively laughter and song.

II

Years of plant life which had struggled to
Grow, now sickens, then dies blackened,
Change again to struggle, sicken
Less, each generation stronger.

Once a city of last millennium,
Now a gentle glen of tall trees
And shallow pool, home to a new
Kinder and healthier human race.

Wars occur only in bad dreams
Of mysterious, distant past.
Village Seers, mind-to-mind
Link together each community.

In Far Vision, Man Do Lin sees
In deepest space the maiden
Voyage of a strange flying ship.
Heavenly balls of fire injure it.

From farthest shore, the doomed ship
Hurtles toward sleepy sylvan
Pearl. Its crew works quickly
To save their royal daughter.

Food, shelter, clothes placed in
Escape launch for the precious
Living jewel, lovely A'maresh.   11/18/91
She is sent towards new destiny.   Revised 07/12/12

Now a Gentle Glen

Quiet, Still-Life Doll

<u>Next to Melting Chariot</u>

A dream of A'maresh,
Her beauty unworldly.
Hair bright from sun's
Droplets upon the earth.

Smooth skin, rich as finest
Cream which flows from our
Heaven's Milky Way. Eyes
Deep blue of night's dome.

Threads of summer sky woven
To frame her classic form,
Curves and folds implied and
Flattered by jeweled patterns.

Not moving, she sits by tree
Next to melting chariot which
Brought her from certain doom
In black graveyard of deepest space.

Dazed from her frantic escape,
Quiet, still-life doll. She
Awaits her awakening to start
A new life in a strange land.

II

Man Do Lin, young woodsman of
Humanity's new race, rides by
In his hunt for forest game.
He stops by clear, cool pool.

Rippling face of loveliness
Touches his hand as he sips.
Almost he falls into the water
Meant for drink, not washing.

He drowns in those laughing
Eyes, his breath forgotten.
He hears the beating of only
One heart, no longer his own.

Hunger rumbles within, not
Only his own appetite. Foods
Unknown to him before crowd
His mind, vivid in their taste.

Answers to her needs bubble up
To his consciousness. Alien and
Man begin their earnest search,
Successful harvest slowly gathered.

11/18/91
Revised 3/05/05

By Clear, Cool Pool

Spun Metal Towers

Metal Drops Never Falling

He looks into her mind
As she sleeps, beckoned
By her thoughts, invited
To learn of her old world.

Man Do Lin, Village Seer,
Rides the mental zephyrs of
A'maresh to graceful world
Of spun metal towers that

Float in gold and purple skies,
Metal drops never falling, always
Singing of A'maresh. Her people,
The brave, happy and wise Andra.

Quiet ships sail golden clouds
From one tower grand to another.
Carriers of goods and people,
Ready to launch soon after arrival.

Mind's intimate touch natural to
All, mentality is greatest treasure.
Mere thought brings desired object
Within reach, fulfills slightest need.

II

From farthest shore voyage begins,
Huge urban sphere, powered
By unimagined energy, tiny
Bubble upon celestial sea.

A'maresh steps into the free-fall
Tube, her strong mind balances
Forces of lift and fall, directs
Distance and speed she travels.

Goddess of the Andran sky, she
Surveys the many galleries
Around her as she rises past.
Her twelfth-level mind works

On several projects at once—the
Length of her worldly journey,
The time already spent and yet to
Come, her state dinner, and more.

Man Do Lin sees himself appear to
Her in a fierce vision or perhaps
A soft daydream while A'maresh
Travels still among the distant seas.

11/19/91
Revised 3/05/05

Free Fall Tube

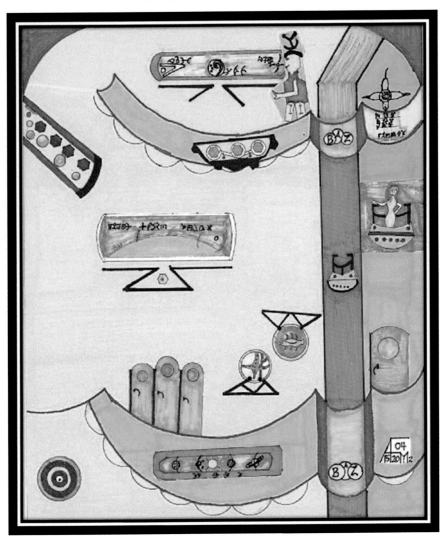

Peaceful, Blue World

Dead of Night

Tiny points of light shower
Fragile artificial globe in
Cold dead of night, afar from
All hope of timely rescue.

A'maresh shudders in woodsman's
Bed asleep, face bathed in sweat.
Man Do Lin feels anxious assault
On his mind by memory vivid of

Her past horror. Repair-bots,
Brave, overwhelmed, cannot fix
Entire damage. Compartments
Sealed, escape ships quickly

Prepared to depart. One withdraws
Safely, A'maresh inside. Exhaustion
Blunts sharp edge of shock over swift
Loss of her family and many friends.

Hurled toward distant sylvan shore
Near one star, not two like her
Own. Peaceful green and blue
Glade, unknown to her people.

II

She awakens, smiles, her nose
Alerted to bubbling, hot broth.
Vegetables and roots merrily
Whirl through mad, boiling sea.

His recent presence in her mind
Welcome with tragic ordeal shared.
Pleasant, rich odor from his pot,
Enough to analyze ingredients found

Within, to heal further her weary,
Weakened body. Covers rapidly slide
Off as she stands innocently before him,
Naked in her perfect, stunning beauty.

Ample but firm her bosom. Lean,
Yet supple her stomach. Well-formed
Her hips. Slight brown forest carpets
Floor between gently tapered legs.

Curves graceful from shoulders down
To plush, round backside. With her
Gracious curtsy for his appreciation,
She reforms woven sky quick as thought.

11/20/91
Revised 3/05/05

Curves Graceful

Curiosity Became the Best of Her

Found in Broken, Blackened Vessel

The serum was found in broken,
Blackened vessel by forest glen.
Pan Do Rae discovered it
In her travels far and wide.

When she encountered the lost ship,
The wise and noble Village Seer's
Curiosity became the best of her.
Caution for the mysteries fled her.

Carefully, however, she entered
To discover what treasures might
Remain within. Twisted metal,
Crumpled circuit boards deterred her not.

Within the darkened interior disarray,
She spied a flash of intense light.
Something made of glittery glass
Attracted her immediate attention.

A label only she could understand
Said, "Andran wasting sickness serum."
Made her wonder what she had found.
Who could this vial of death harm?

II

Engaging in Far Vision, she probed
The precious object in her hand.
A complicated scenario, of ancient past,
Was revealed to her perspicacity.

From a star in Andran sky the virus
Fell to hurt the unsuspecting people.
Only a family of healers, who
Took the illness for themselves,

Could help the wasting many.
They died so that others might live.
After many years of this scourge
A prophecy of good fortune.

The promise of a future:
From the family into which
A'maresh was born, a new
Healer would find a cure.

How did the lovely A'maresh
Forget her trusteeship of the vial?
The answer: the new world
Discoveries that she made.

Precious Object in Her Hand

Kindly Mental Touch

Festival of Welcome

Love's sweet flower blooms in
Man Do Lin's cottage. Village
Seer and woodsman, he shares his
Home and all his worldly wisdom

Gladly with celestial beauty
A'maresh. Forest creatures and
Those of air feel kindly mental
Touch of curious explorers two.

His eyes open in an owl's stare,
She walks the grass in a snake's
Slither. Each laugh with the sight
Of the other's attempts to be an animal.

When the Seers touch mind-to-mind in
Far Vision, distant news is given
About Man Do Lin's discovery of
Alien A'maresh and her recovery.

Plans quickly form among the Seers
To come all together in Festival of
Welcome, to introduce and accept
The rare occasion of a woman Seer.

I Dream of A'maresh

II

Clowns gay, jugglers deft, acrobats
Flying, bright stalls of food drink
Crisscross jolly Farmer Kris To Fer's
Great meadow. Popcorn buttery and

Candy sugar-spun feed
Children running, who carry
Balloons to color the cloudless sky.
On grand display sits A'maresh.

Raised high above one and all, on
Platform skirted in gold and blue,
Amidst four from the Seers Council,
She receives courtesy and gifts

From her peers of Far Vision.
Jewels, vestments and other finery
Presented humbly along with
Approving touch of gentle minds.

The final Seer, Pan Do Rae, perceived
As the wisest, conceals her envy--and fatal
Andran disease—inside a jewel-encrusted box.
Yet bright A'maresh knows the gift's truth.

11/21/91
Revised 07/12/12

On Grand Display

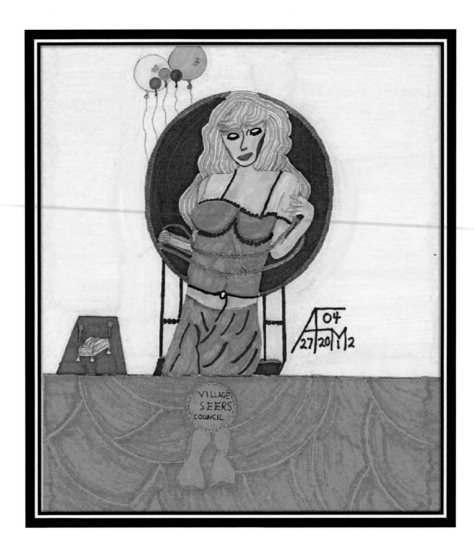

A Place to Find Books

<u>Before Fiery Rebirth</u>

Festival's fond memories recede
In the year of happiness Man Do Lin
Shares with his gentle A'maresh.
They often explore the far countryside.

His small library enlightens her of this new world's
Wonders. Though the books are few in number,
The scope of knowledge intrigues. Her genuine
Thirst to learn still more of period before world's

Fiery rebirth is now whetted. Man Do Lin
Reveals there is a place to find
Other books of science and learning.
A'maresh is eager to find them soon.

Provisions prepared for journey long—
Food, water, sturdy clothes
For days ahead, strong shelter for their
Nights away. On horses, they set forth.

Past Village North, through Forest
Redwood to its very edge before the
Valley Grand—with its wild fruits, grains,
Roots and vegetables in lush array.

II

In Valley Grand, a wide, ancient cracked stairway
Is hidden from public view by a full orchard of
Apple trees that blankets an opening—a hole
Framed by four statues tall and broad of concrete.

Two horses snort, stamp nervously
Near opening to tomb of learning.
Armed with sword and cold lamp of
Fireflies, bold Man Do Lin leads

A'maresh with her cold lamp and
Sword through pale caverns of
Molding canvas and long-since
Broken glass and metal doors.

But from tiny fragment of colored
Tapestry, her brilliant mind sees
Ancient scenes of battles and their
Heroes. Her imagination bombarded

By events public and private. Dark
Halls now light up within her mind.
School girl again, she runs to every
Room. Everywhere her laughter echoes.

11/23/91
Revised 3/05/05

She Runs to Every Room

Deep In Urban Temple

__Every Frontier Explored__

Through careful search for books
In unblemished condition, World's
New daughter and mature son gather
The wild oats of humankind's past

Learning. Before the winds from
Giant mushroom cloud purified the
Planet with its long-lived death
Outspread, a great and frenzied

Race seemed ready to embrace its
Own end. Their every frontier
Explored, all knowledge had been
Tapped to be recorded in printed

Nutmeat secure, stored for future
Human squirrels burrowing. Canvas
Bags full-laden, happy A'maresh and
Man Do Lin prepare to return home.

Deep in urban temple of books, she hastily
Places a tiny sparkling box—Pan Do Rae's
"Gift"—in empty, broken glass case of some
Musty, darkened, unnamed room behind her.

Lovely A'maresh wishes to conceal deadly
Box from hands innocent or dangerous.
It is her hope that no one visits secret room in
Buried edifice of treasured books from ancient past.

II

Another year of continued happiness
Passes for the woodsman and his lovely
Guest. Seers Council learns of wedding
Plans for their Man Do Lin and his

Stunning bride-to-be A'maresh. The
Farmer Kris To Fer offers his grand
Meadow for their marriage festival
And bridal pavilion for First Night.

In Desolate Wood, only other woman
Seer, Pan Do Rae, jealousy incarnate
And spite-filled, looks with her Far
Vision to joyous provisions made.

Her illusion of breadfruit home,
Roofed in icing, ginger bread interior
With strawberry jam windows entices
Little children to visit. From their

Skins she makes her walls and other
Furnishings. Her furniture is built
From young bones, upholstered from
Kitten hides—unknown to the Council.

Their trust in Pan Do Rae is such that
They seek her out for a special delight.
At their innocent request she bakes   11/23/91
A rich wedding cake—to kill them all!   07/12/12
                                             (Revised)

Built From Young Bones

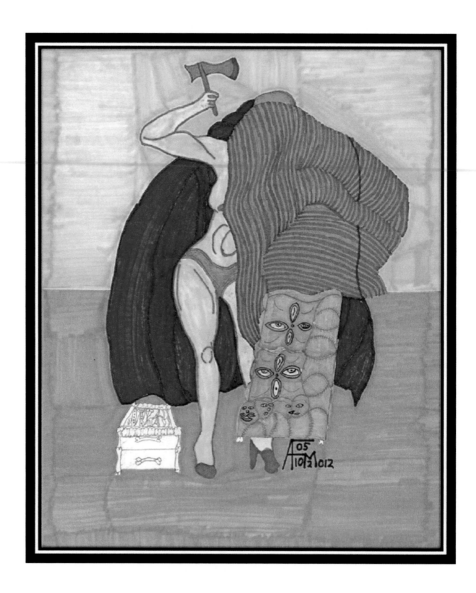

Bright with Banners

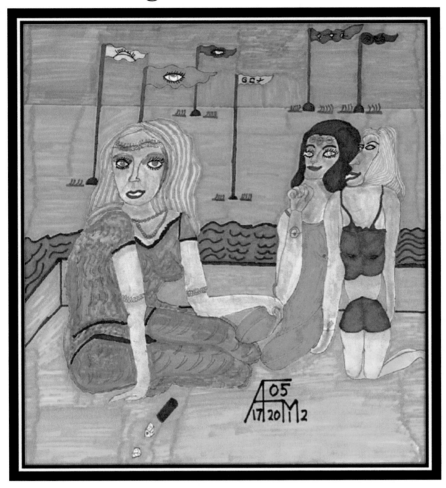

<u>The River Aciton—Banners Bright</u>

"I, Cam O'Lin, brother to Village
Seer and today's happy groom,
Watched the boats reach River
Aciton's shore at jolly Farmer

Kris To Fer's great meadow. The
Village Seers and all their large
Retinues arrived on twenty barges,
Bright with colorful banners.

The waters rippled with much commotion
Of such joyous throng. Guests come to
Join uniting of proud Man Do Lin and his
Sweet, blushing bride, beautiful A'maresh.

He, a handsome woodsman dressed
In crimson and peacock vest over
Rich cream ruffled shirt and pleated
Snow-white pants, matched by kid's

Skin boots and high-plumed hat. His
Tie is made from pressed roses. She,
A lovely woman from the heavens, in sky
Blue veil, sheer chiffon gown of starry night."

II

"I, Cam O'Lin, delighted in the joy of my
Brother at the sight of A'maresh, her
Gown lit by jewels bright, rainbow-colored.
I then watched Pan Do Rae land with the

Wedding cake on her gilded barge. Before
Appearance of A'maresh blessed our fair
Land, Pan was solitary woman Seer and
Wisest of all: She revealed the places

Hidden of the father race, unlocked
Their code of writing, practiced
Their healing art, and disclosed
The Ritual Journey for a Life-Mate.

Now tragic misfortune struck her
River-borne party. A small, swift
Boat with careless drive ran
Straight into the slow barge, upsetting

Five-tiered wedding cake, which
Toppled into river. To horrified
Eyes of Pan Do Rae and assembled
Crowd, river boiled blood rose.

Witnesses speculated at horrible
State of River Aciton: Who could   11/28/91
Have spoiled the lustrous cake? Poor   07/12/12
Pan Do Rae seemed as surprised as anyone."   (Revised)

Upset Wedding Cake

The Joining of These Two Souls

To You A Child Is Born

In the bridal pavilion on First Night
The suddenly gentle woodsman
Man Do Lin took his fair, sweet
A'maresh to their wedding bed.

With just their quiet, unassuming
Thoughts, each removed the
Other's colorful garment to
Reveal the glory that was theirs.

Two rushing waves crashed upon
Parched seashores, flooding in
A calm tidal pool of pure,
Scorching, loving embrace.

The joining of these two souls
Was the caress of the Andran sky
Over the welcoming fields of
Man Do Lin's sylvan glen.

With this night's joining of woodsman
And heavenly woman is a child to be born.
A tiny miracle seed is planted tonight,
Surpassing all the jewels worn by A'maresh.

II

But elsewhere, not to be outdone, Pan Do Rae,
When her Far Vision reveals A'maresh's state,
Courts her own husband, the naïve
Farmer Kris To Fer, to his especial delight.

Yet Pan Do Rae has a secret dire which
She dare not reveal to her unsuspecting
Groom. He marries her with the seed
Of another man within her womb.

But after the child so conceived is weaned
From his mother's nursing breast, she claims
That pressing affairs of state keep her too
Occupied to raise him herself.

Poor besotted Kris To Fer is pushed
To find a nanny and then a governess
To bring up a dignified and well-behaved
Young lad of whom his father can be proud.

To Man Do Lin and A'maresh a darling
As'gareth is born. In beauty she shows
Charms similar to her delighted mother.
Her mind is as keen as each of theirs.

The child of Kris and Pan is young
Da Vid Son (a name she chose to
Taunt her husband), born of a lover   03/05/05
She dare not acknowledge in marriage.   07/12/12
                                                    (Revised)

The Child of Kris and Pan

A Sense of Connectedness

<u>Two Peas From Different Pods</u>

Growing up, As'gareth, always outgoing,
Has many young friends with whom she
Laughs and plays many games. They
Love to run around in her big yard.

Always in gentle touch with her parents,
Mind-to-mind, she forever feels loved.
She would always be ready to help an
Animal in need of a Healing Touch.

Her experience with her limited Far
Vision, nurtured by her parents,
Gives her a sense of connectedness
To a larger world outside herself.

She just *knew* that all living things
Come from the same source, an
Over-Soul, and injury to the least
Of His creatures saddened Him.

As she grows older, she learns the importance
Of a Ritual Journey for a Life-Mate for herself.
And it is the story of her loving parents
Wedding that she wants to hear before she goes.

II

Da Vid Son is most like his father Kris in nature,
But he has a mind much like his mother also.
His friends are mostly the characters in the
Books from which his governess taught him.

His concept about his mother is mostly an ideal.
He knows her only in the abstract—one of two women
Seers on the Council, the Wisest of the Council,
Mistress of the ancient language and healing arts.

He knows about the Over-Soul, but only from books.
He accepts the sacred writings that tell of His existence
And the Laws that govern His Path.
But he isn't sure that he is following the teachings.

As'gareth and Da Vid Son are two peas
From different pods, but both of good stock.
They don't know it yet, but their destinies
Are intertwined, two vines reaching upwards.

The same sun nurtures both plants.
One a child of nature and the World
Itself. And the other a student of letters
Studying the Ideal in the abstract.

03/17/05

Their Destiny Is Entwined

---To Be Continued---

In Book II

Made in the USA
Middletown, DE
23 August 2015